Scholastic

# Clifford

# CLIFFORD'S LOOSE TOOTH

Adapted by Wendy Cheyette Lewison

Illustrated by John and Sandrina Kurtz

## Based on the Scholastic book series
## "Clifford The Big Red Dog"
## by Norman Bridwell

Cartwheel
·B·O·O·K·S·®

### SCHOLASTIC INC.

New York   Toronto   London   Auckland   Sydney   Mexico City
New Delhi   Hong Kong   Buenos Aires

No part of this publication may be reproduced, or stored in a retrieval system, or transmitted in any form or by any means, electronic, mechanical, photocopying, recording, or otherwise, without written permission of the publisher. For information regarding permission, write to Scholastic Inc., Attention: Permissions Department, 555 Broadway, New York, NY 10012.

ISBN 0-439-33245-1

Library of Congress Cataloging-in-Publication Data available

20 19 18 17 16                                06

Printed in the U.S.A.    23
First printing, February 2002

Clifford was happy.

He had a nice big bone

to chew on.

All of a sudden,

he stopped chewing.

"Uh-oh," he said.

"My tooth is loose."

Clifford had never felt

a loose tooth before.

It wiggled.

It wobbled.

He was worried.

"Don't worry, Clifford,"

said Emily Elizabeth.

"It's just a loose puppy tooth.

When it falls out,

a new one will grow in its place."

"See?" said Emily Elizabeth.

"I have some new teeth!"

Emily Elizabeth went into the house.

She came out with a box.

In the box was a shiny quarter.

"The Tooth Fairy took my old tooth,"

said Emily Elizabeth.

"She left this for me

under my pillow."

Clifford looked at the beautiful,

shiny quarter.

Maybe he would get a treat

from the Tooth Fairy, too!

Off he went to tell
Cleo and T-Bone.

"Hmm," said Cleo.
"I bet we can help that
tooth along a little bit."

"How can we do that?"

asked Clifford.

"We can just pull it out!"

said Cleo.

"I don't think so…"

said Clifford.

"You could sneeze it out,"

said T-Bone.

"On the other hand…

Mrs. Bleakman might not
like that so much."

"Maybe you could chew

some bubble gum,"

said Cleo.

"A LOT of bubble gum.

Lots and lots and lots!"

Clifford thought about

chewing bubble gum.

He thought about the bubble

he would blow—

bigger and bigger and bigger.

*Pop!* went the bubble.

What a mess!

"Thank you for your ideas,"
Clifford said to his friends.

Then Clifford waited

for his tooth to come out

all by itself.

It was hard to wait.

But one day,

out it came!

That night, Clifford put

the tooth under his pillow.

In the morning, Clifford

found a very big treat

from the Tooth Fairy…

who gave Clifford's tooth

to Mr. and Mrs. Howard

for The Seashell shop.

Now everyone could see

Clifford's big tooth!

# Do You Remember?

**Circle the right answer.**

1. When Clifford felt his loose tooth, he was chewing on…

    a. a bug.

    b. a bone.

    c. a ball.

2. Cleo and _____ thought of ways to help Clifford's tooth come out early.

    a. Mac

    b. Charley

    c. T-Bone

**Which happened first?**
**Which happened next?**
**Which happened last?**
**Write a 1, 2, or 3 in the space after each sentence.**

The Tooth Fairy gave Clifford a bone. _____

Emily Elizabeth showed Clifford her quarter. _____

Clifford imagined blowing a very big bubble. _____

**Answers:**

Clifford imagined blowing a very big bubble. (2)

Emily Elizabeth showed Clifford her quarter. (1)

The Tooth Fairy gave Clifford a bone. (3)

2. c

1. b